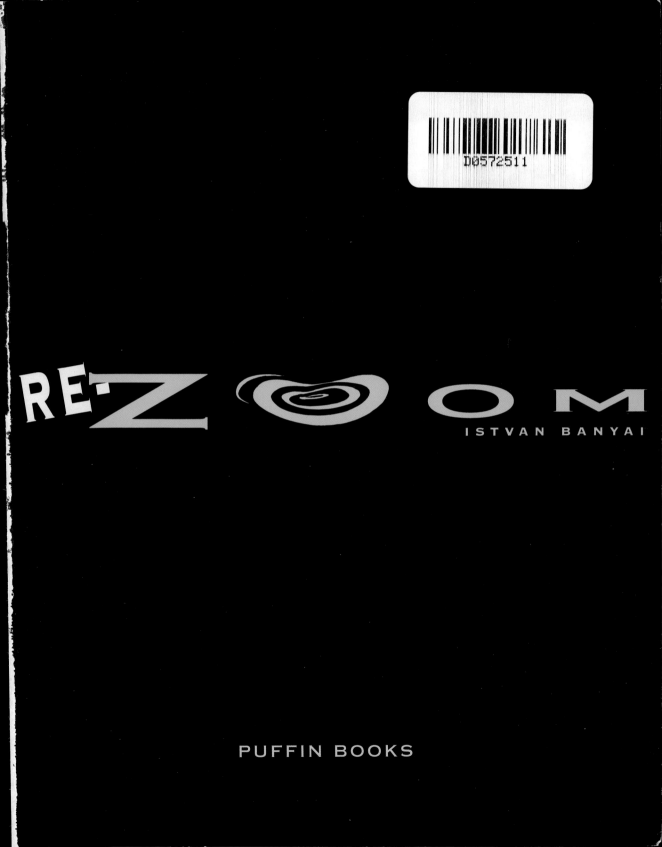

RE-ZOOM

ISTVAN BANYAI

PUFFIN BOOKS

WITH SPECIAL THANKS TO
REGINA, BECKY, DAPHNE, MARGARET & NINA

PUFFIN BOOKS
PUBLISHED BY THE PENGUIN GROUP
PENGUIN PUTNAM INC., 345 HUDSON STREET, NEW YORK, NEW YORK 10014, U.S.A.
PENGUIN BOOKS LTD, 27 WRIGHTS LANE, LONDON W8 5TZ, ENGLAND
PENGUIN BOOKS AUSTRALIA LTD, RINGWOOD, VICTORIA, AUSTRALIA
PENGUIN BOOKS CANADA LTD, 10 ALCORN AVENUE, TORONTO, ONTARIO, CANADA M4V 3B2
PENGUIN BOOKS (N.Z.) LTD, 182-190 WAIRAU ROAD, AUCKLAND 10, NEW ZEALAND

PENGUIN BOOKS LTD, REGISTERED OFFICES: HARMONDSWORTH, MIDDLESEX, ENGLAND

FIRST PUBLISHED IN THE UNITED STATES OF AMERICA BY VIKING,
A DIVISION OF PENGUIN BOOKS USA INC., 1995
PUBLISHED BY PUFFIN BOOKS, A MEMBER OF PENGUIN PUTNAM BOOKS FOR YOUNG READERS, 1998

21 22 23 24 25 26 27 28 29 30

THE LIBRARY OF CONGRESS HAS CATALOGED THE VIKING EDITION AS FOLLOWS:
BANYAI, ISTVAN.
RE-ZOOM / BY ISTVAN BANYAI.   P.   CM.
SUMMARY: A WORDLESS PICTURE BOOK PRESENTS A SERIES OF SCENES, EACH ONE FROM FARTHER
AWAY, SHOWING, FOR EXAMPLE, A BOAT WHICH BECOMES THE IMAGE ON A
MAGAZINE, WHICH IS HELD IN A HAND, WHICH BELONGS TO A BOY, AND SO ON.
ISBN 0-670-86392-0
[1. VISUAL PERCEPTION—FICTION. 2. STORIES WITHOUT WORDS.] I. TITLE.
PZ7.B22947RE 1995 [E]—DC20 95-14265 CIP AC

PUFFIN BOOKS ISBN 978-0-14-055694-0

MANUFACTURED IN CHINA